Stories to Read by Yourself

Written and illustrated by Sue Camm

BRIMAX BOOKS · NEWMARKET · ENGLAND

Tinka Elephant's Nose

Tinka the baby elephant
lives in Africa.
It is very hot there, but
Tinka's home is in a cool
and shady forest.
Tinka has a very long nose.
It is called a trunk.
All elephants have trunks.
Tinka likes to play
in the forest.

To. BETHAN.
from. GRAN & GRANDAD HOUGHTON
Xmas 1992.

Contents

ISBN 0 86112 938 5

© Brimax Books Ltd 1988. All rights reserved.
This edition first published by
Brimax Books Ltd, Newmarket, England 1992.
Printed in Portugal.

Mick Monkey makes fun
of Tinka Elephant.
"You do look funny!
My nose is neat and flat,
so I do not bump it when
I climb the trees," he says.
Mick jumps onto a branch
and swings by his tail.
"Maybe my nose is too
long," says Tinka.

Poll Parrot makes fun
of Tinka Elephant.
"You do look funny! I have
a hard beak. I can crack
nuts open with my beak,"
says Poll Parrot.
Then, Poll spreads her
wings and flies away.
"I am sure my nose is too
long," says Tinka.

Little Wild Pig makes fun
of Tinka Elephant.
"You do look funny! My
nose is short and strong.
I can dig up nice roots
to eat. Look, like this."
He digs with his nose in
the soft ground.
"Now I know my nose is
too long!" says Tinka.

Tiny Giraffe makes fun
of Tinka Elephant.
"You do look funny! I have
a short black nose. Your
nose is so long it must
get in the way when you
run!" says Tiny Giraffe.
Then, he flicks his tail
and runs into the forest.
"I wish I had a short nose
like Tiny," says
Tinka Elephant.

"The animals make fun of my long nose," says Tinka to her mother. "Can I make my trunk grow short?"
"You are silly," says her mother. "A long nose is a great help to an elephant. Just wait and see!
Now go and play so I can have a sleep."

Tinka plays by the river.
Mick Monkey is on the
other side of the river.
"How can I cross over?" he
says. "I cannot swim!"
"Wait, I can help you,"
says Tinka.
See how she helps Mick to
cross the river.
"I am sorry I made fun of
your nose. It is
a great help!"

Who is this in the river?
Splash! Splash!
"Help!" says Poll Parrot.
"Get me out of the water!"
See how Tinka pulls her out.
"Thank you," says Poll.
"I fell in when I was
washing my tail. Your trunk
has saved me. I am glad
that you have a long nose!"

Tinka and her new friends
meet Little Wild Pig as
he digs up some roots.
"The best root goes under
this heavy log. I cannot
dig it up," he says.
Tinka can help. See how
she moves the heavy log.
"I will not make fun of
your nose again," says
Little Wild Pig
as he runs away.

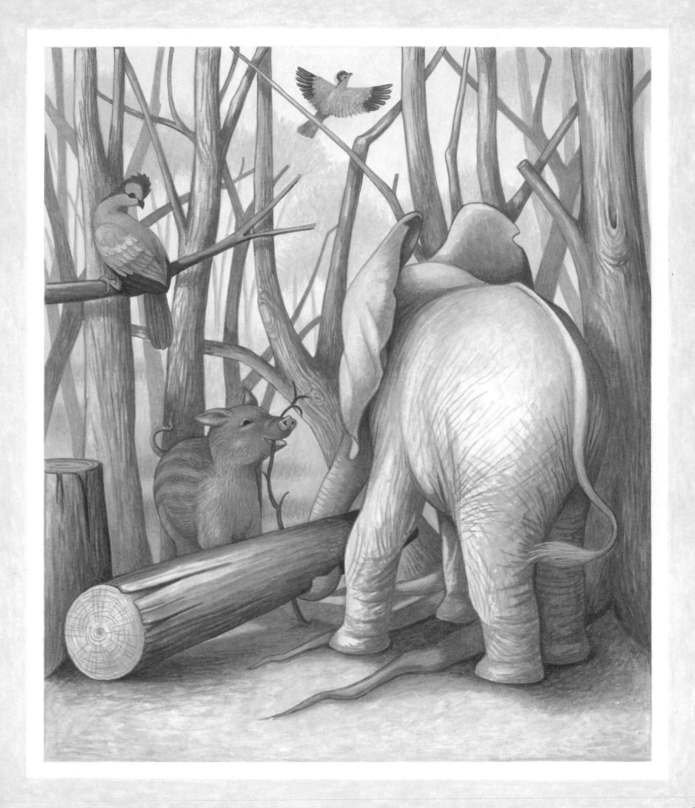

Tiny Giraffe needs help.
"I like to eat new green
leaves. The best ones are
at the top of the tree.
But I am not big yet and
I cannot get them."
"I can get them for you,"
says Tinka. See how she
picks the new green leaves.
"A long nose can be a
great help after
all!" says Tinka.

Tinka sniffs the air.
"What a funny smell!"
she says.
Poll Parrot can see a long
way. "Smoke!" she says.
"There is a fire in the forest.
What can we do?"
Tinka knows what to do.
She puts her trunk in the
air. She calls to all the
elephants in
the forest.

Mother Elephant and all
the big elephants come
to help.
"We must get water to put
out the fire!" says Tinka.
The elephants go to the
river and they suck lots
of water into their trunks.
See how they put out
the fire.

The fire is out and the
forest is safe again.
"Hurray!" say Mick Monkey
and Poll Parrot.
"Hurray!" say Little Wild
Pig and Tiny Giraffe.
"Three cheers for all the
elephants!" they say.
"Three cheers for Tinka
the Elephant's nose!"

Say these words again

elephant	giraffe
monkey	parrot
shady	flicks
climb	swings
branch	crack
leaves	hurray
cheers	splash
spreads	heavy
friends	washing
other	mother

How does Tinka help her friends?

Diggy Mole's New Home

Diggy is a mole. His coat
is black and soft. He can
dig in the ground with
his strong front claws.
He digs a long tunnel under
the field by the river.
This is where Diggy lives
in a cosy home at the end
of the tunnel. When the
sun shines, Diggy Mole
loves to sit and
look at the river.

Today, Diggy wakes up with
wet feet. When he jumps
out of bed he lands in a
puddle.
Splash!
Plop, plop, plop he goes
along to his front door.
He looks outside.
"What can I do now?
I know what this is.
It is a flood!"
says Diggy.

The water from the river
has made a flood in his
field.

"Look what the flood has
done to my cosy home! This
is very bad. I must find
a new home to live in,"
says poor Diggy.

The water is not very deep.
He can make his way right
across the field
to the hedge.

Diggy must look for a new home away from the water. "A blackbird lives high up in the hedge," says Diggy. "It will not be wet there. A bird's nest is just what I need."
Diggy looks in the hedge until he finds an empty bird's nest. He climbs in. "I will be dry here," he says.

When night comes, Diggy
cannot sleep. The moon and
the stars are too bright.
"I do not want to live in
a home without a roof,"
says Diggy.
In the morning, he jumps
out of the bird's nest in
the hedge.
Diggy goes along the lane.
"What can I do?"
says poor Diggy.

Diggy begins to look for
a new home with a roof.
He meets a fat brown toad.
The toad says, "Come and
have a bite to eat with me."
He goes into Toad's home.
"If you want a home with
a roof, why not have
this flowerpot? I am
moving out today. You
can move in,"
says the toad.

When night comes, Diggy
cannot sleep. A flowerpot
home has cold walls.
The hole in the bottom
lets in the wind.
"I have never been so cold!"
says Diggy Mole.
"I do not want to live in
a cold home like this,"
says Diggy. Off he goes
down the lane
into a farmyard.

Diggy begins to look for
a new home that is warm.
He sees Mother Hen with
all her little chicks.
"Mother Hen takes care to
keep her chicks snug and
warm," says Diggy Mole.
"I can make a cosy home in
the henhouse. I can make
it with some straw." So then,
Diggy makes a
nice warm home.

When night comes, Diggy
cannot sleep. All the hens
begin to snore. All the
little chicks run about
after bedtime. They do not
want to go to bed.
Diggy is very very cross.
"I cannot stay here,"
says Diggy Mole.
In the morning, he goes
out and across
the cornfield.

Diggy begins to look for
a new home where no one
wakes him up at night.
He sees a big tree by the
side of the cornfield.
"This is just what I want,"
says Diggy Mole.
"I can make a home in the
roots of that tree. No one
will wake me up there."
Diggy begins to
make a new home.

When night comes, Diggy cannot sleep. There is not a sound. He is all alone. Diggy feels afraid.

"I do not like to be alone," says Diggy. "I must go away from here." In the morning, he gets up. He goes away from the tree. He goes along a sandy bank.

He is very sad.

What can he do?

Diggy sees a little door
in the sandy bank. "Here
is a tunnel just like mine!"
he says. He looks inside.
Someone is coming along
the tunnel. It is someone
who has a soft black coat.
"Hello, I am Monty Mole,"
he says. "Come inside.
I live all by myself.
I am so glad to meet you."
Diggy goes into
the tunnel.

"The water made a flood in my home. I cannot find a new home," says poor Diggy. "A mole needs a tunnel and a cosy home to live in."
"It is great fun to share," says Monty. "You can have my spare room!"
"Hurray! Thank you, Monty!" says Diggy. "Now I have a new home and a new friend too!"

Say these words again

claws	bright
tunnel	toad
field	flowerpot
puddle	henhouse
splash	straw
flood	cornfield
warm	someone
hedge	myself
blackbird	sound
empty	coming

Whose homes are these?

Ben Bear's Pot of Gold

Ben, the little brown bear,
wants to go out to play.
"You cannot go out in the
rain," says Mother Bear.
She looks to see if the
clouds have gone away.
"Ben!" she says. "Look at
the rainbow in the sky."
The rainbow goes all the
way to the Misty Hills.
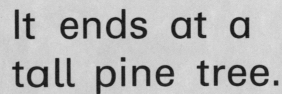 It ends at a
tall pine tree.

"There is a story about a rainbow," says Mother Bear. "At the end of a rainbow there is a pot of gold." "Our rainbow ends at the tall pine tree," says Ben. "What fun! I can go to look for gold in the Misty Hills. I can look for it by the tall pine tree."

Ben sets off with a picnic box. It is full of good things to eat.

"Hello! Are you going to have a picnic?" says Bob the beaver.

"No," says Ben. "I am off to the Misty Hills. I want to find the pot of gold at the end of the rainbow."

"I will come too!" says Bob.

Ben and Bob set off down
the path. They meet
Skipper the chipmunk.
"We are on our way to the
Misty Hills," says Ben.
"There is a pot of gold
at the end of the rainbow.
We are going to find it,
by the tall pine tree."
"What fun!" says Skipper.
"Wait for me,
I will come too!"

Ben, Bob and Skipper
follow the path to the
Misty Hills.
"We are off to look for
gold by the tall pine
tree," sings Ben.
"We will find the pot
of gold," sings Bob.
Meg the magpie hears them.
"What fun!" she says.

"Wait for me,
I will come too!"

It is a very long way
to the Misty Hills.
They stop at a pond to
drink. Bob the beaver
has a swim.
"This is a lovely pond to
swim in," he says.
"Swimming is what I like
to do best of all."
"We can call it Bob's Pond,"
says Ben. "But
now we must go."

They have a long way to go
so they rest in the forest.
Skipper finds an old log.
"This would make a lovely
house," he says.
"The best kind of house
for a chipmunk is inside
an old log."
"We can call it Skipper's
Log," says Ben.

"But now we
must go on."

They all go along the path
to the Misty Hills.
"Where is Meg the magpie?"
"Here I am," says Meg.
"Look what I have found.
Red berries! I do love
red berries."
She eats until she is full.
"We can call this Meg's
Berry Place," says Ben.

"But now we
must go on."

Skipper, Bob and Meg
go along the path
to the Misty Hills.
Is Ben lost?
No, here he is with a
very sticky face!
"I have found a bees' nest
full of honey," he says.
"We can call it Ben's Honey
Place," says Bob.
"But now we
must go on."

The path goes up a hill.
The ground is hard and
full of rocks and stones.
"We are in the Misty Hills,"
says Ben. "There is the tall
pine tree. That is where
I saw the rainbow end.
That is where we have
to go to find the pot
of gold."

They go to the tall pine
tree and look for the
pot of gold.
"There is nothing up here,"
says Meg the magpie.
"Nothing down here,"
says Bob the beaver.
"Nothing here at all!"
says Skipper sadly.
Ben is sad too, but he
says, "Never
mind the gold . . .

... Bob has found a lovely pond to swim in.
Skipper has found a new log house to live in.
Meg has found lots of nice berries to eat.
I have found a store full of sweet honey.
We have all found our own pot of gold!"

They are all very happy.
They make a camp fire and
sit round it. They eat the
food from the picnic box.
"It is a long way home,"
says Ben, "but it was fun
to go to the end of the
rainbow!"
Do you think there is a
pot of gold at the end of
the rainbow?
Maybe there is.

Say these words again

little	brown
Mother	clouds
rainbow	story
picnic	things
beaver	chipmunk
wait	follow
magpie	swimming
lovely	sticky
where	nothing
misty	Hello